WORLD WAR II TALES
THE BARREL BURGLARY

First published 2015 by
A & C Black, an imprint of Bloomsbury Publishing Plc
50 Bedford Square
London WC1B 3DP

www.bloomsbury.com

Bloomsbury is a registered trademark of Bloomsbury Publishing Plc

Text copyright © 2015 Terry Deary
Illustrations copyright © 2015 James de la Rue

The rights of Terry Deary and James de la Rue to be identified as the
author and illustrator of this work have been asserted by them in
accordance with the Copyrights, Designs and Patents Act 1988.

ISBN 978-1-4729-1627-3

A CIP catalogue for this book is available from the British Library.

Printed and bound by CPI Group (UK) Ltd, Croydon CR0 4YY

1 3 5 7 9 10 8 6 4 2

MIX
Paper from
responsible sources
FSC® C020471
www.fsc.org

WORLD WAR II TALES

TERRY DEARY

THE BARREL BURGLARY

Illustrated by James de la Rue

A & C BLACK
AN IMPRINT OF BLOOMSBURY
LONDON   NEW DELHI   NEW YORK   SYDNEY

Chapter 1

Barbed wire and body-bits

1941 – Sunderland in the North-East of England

Jack Burn's granddad was 55 years old, and that was too old to fight in the war. 'I could still fight you know,' he told Jack that morning.

Jack sighed. 'I know.' Granddad said that just about every morning.

'In the last war, the Great War, I was a sergeant. Colonel Morris said I was the best sergeant in the Durham Light Infantry.

The best. My men were the smartest, the bravest, and they shot straight as this poker,' the old man went on.

He pulled the poker out of the fire. It was glowing orange and he used the tip to light his pipe.

'The poker's bent,' Jack said. The boy's thin, pointed nose twitched as the smell of burning tobacco crept into his nostrils.

His ears were small but they stuck out a long way from his head. His short-cropped hair made them look like jug handles.

The man sucked on his pipe and smacked his lips. 'Ah, that's better.' He sat back in the worn old armchair and watched the blue smoke drift up to the ceiling of the kitchen.

'Of course in the Great War we spent a lot of time sitting in trenches. Now in *this* war they are charging around in aeroplanes and tanks, jumping with parachutes and attacking on landing craft from the sea.'

Jack sighed, 'I know,' again. He had seen the barbed wire strung along the beach to stop the enemy running up the promenade and into the town. Jack knew it was the shipyards they wanted to attack— 'Stop the ships and you stop the food

getting in and you starve Britain,' his mate Tommy Crawley said. Tommy couldn't read or write but he knew more than the grown-ups.

And Jack knew about bombs. The enemy were trying to smash the shipyards a mile away, but a lot of the bombs missed the yards and hit the houses. There was a gap in Robinson Terrace that Jack and Tommy walked past on their way to school. It was like a gap in Granddad's mouth when he took his false teeth out at night. The wreckage of three houses had been cleared away but there was still rubble of broken bricks and beams and glass.

'We could play on there,' Jack said one Saturday.

'Not me, mate,' Tommy Crawley hissed. 'They reckon Bella Hudson went down in the cellar when the bombing started. She's still there now... well, bits of her.'

Jack didn't know if he should believe Tommy's tales. But from then on he crossed the road when he walked past the bomb site in Robinson Terrace.

The boy picked up a canvas bag, checked his homework was inside and threw it over his shoulder. 'I'm off to school, Granddad. See you later.'

The man looked through the pipe smoke. 'Don't be late,' he said. 'We have a Home Guard parade tonight.'

Jack grinned suddenly. 'I wouldn't want to miss that,' he said and bounced out of the door. Home Guard parades were great. The men of the district, too old or too young to fight in the war, made their own little army. When the enemy landed they would be met by Granddad's troop of lion-hearts and rabbit-hearts. 'Those invaders will die!' Granddad said.

'They'll die of laughing,' Tommy Crawley would mutter.

Chapter 2
Cows and curtains

School was as boring as ever for Jack. Billy Anderson took a box of matches into the classroom and set fire to a sheet of paper from his exercise book. It smoked in his desk and the smoke came out through the ink-well hole.

Mr Wilson the French teacher was furious. 'There's a war on, Anderson. It is a crime to waste precious paper.' He bent him over the desk and slapped the back of his patched pants with an old gym shoe. Apart from that nothing much happened.

School dinner was stewed beef pie. 'This cow died of old age,' Tommy grumbled as he chewed on the tough meat and spat out the gristle.

When the bell went at four o'clock Jack raced home with Tommy Crawley. 'See you at the Home Guard tonight,' he panted as Tommy ran on.

Granddad was waiting. 'Pop down to the butcher shop and get us a quarter pound of sausage,' he said. 'Here's the coupon.'

Jack ran to the shop on the corner of Fowler Terrace and got three thin links of sawdust-filled sausage from Mrs Jackson. Mr Jackson the butcher was away in Scotland, serving as a cook for the RAF. Jack hoped Mr Jackson's pilots got better sausages than his wife made.

After dinner of sausage and mash and carrot Granddad boiled a pan of water and washed up. Then he went upstairs to change into his uniform while the boy raced through the ten sums he had to do for homework. He scribbled the answers on the corner of yesterday's Sunderland Echo. He'd pass the answers on to Tommy when he saw him.

Granddad's iron-studded boots clattered down the stairs. Jack put a shovel of coal dust on the fire to damp it down and keep it going till they got back. They pulled all the blackout curtains tight shut and stepped out into Robinson Terrace. As they walked past the bomb site Jack asked, 'Are there bits of Auntie Bella in there, Granddad?'

The man looked uncomfortable. 'No, lad.'

'I haven't seen her since the raid last December.'

'She's gone to Whitby down in Yorkshire. Evacuated.'

Jack frowned as he tried to march in step

with the man. 'Only kids get evacuated,' he argued.

'Your Auntie Bella evacuated herself.'

'Can you do that?'

Granddad's face was grim in the fading light. 'I'll evacuate your head if you don't stop asking questions. Now shut up and get in step.'

'Yes, Granddad.'

They marched on in silence to the Saint Barnabas church hall where the Home Guard held their meetings. There were twenty men in uniform there but just two boys—Jack and Tommy. They were allowed there because they had fathers away in the war and no mother at home. They went along with their granddads... so long as they sat in the corner and kept quiet.

Tommy grinned when he saw Jack.

He slipped the homework answers into his trouser pocket and said, 'It'll be fun tonight. They're going to try marching in time.'

Jack returned the grin. The last time the men had done marching one had tripped over his own feet and three others fell on top of him.

Jack's granddad marched into the dusty old hall, saluted the captain and said, 'Ready to lead marching practice, sir.'

'Carry on, Sergeant Burn,' the captain said.

'It'll be a carry on, all right,' Tommy sniggered.

Chapter 3
Barrels and bombs

The marching was ragged as a crow with torn feathers. But no one fell over. Tommy and Jack grew bored.

First the Robinson Terrace Home Guard paraded up and down the hall. Sergeant Burn didn't just shout at them, he barked and bawled and bayed and howled and yowled.

Then they went outside into the moonlit gloom to march around the church block three times. The oldest men were seventy and groaning with tiredness so the captain

called them back inside the hall for a cup
of tea. The boys made themselves useful
by serving the biscuits.

The captain told the men to put the
folding wooden chairs in rows and to sit
on them. When they were settled and
quiet he said, 'Now, men, we have been
preparing to fight off an enemy who will
land on our beaches, or troops who drop
out of the skies.'

Some of the men raised their eyes to the roof and looked a little worried. 'We can't fight the bombs that drop out of the skies,' Granddad grumbled.

'Exactly,' the captain said. 'But while we wait for the invasion we can do more than practise our marching and our shooting. We can help fight the bombing— what they are calling the Blitz. I want your ideas.'

The men looked at the floor. They shuffled their feet. They coughed. Suddenly Granddad pointed at a man in the front row. 'The officer asked you a question. Answer him. A bomb falls. What can we do to help?'

The man shook his head and babbled, 'Clear up the rubble?'

'Very good,' the captain said and the ideas started to flow. Carry stretchers for the wounded. Help old people to the shelters. Get the dogs off the street in case they got scared and started biting people—the troop weren't too sure about that one.

'Put out the fires?' a man said.

'We don't have any hoses and pumps and fire engines,' someone else argued.

'Ahhhh,' the men sighed and went silent again.

Then Tommy spoke up. 'The bombers

drop fire bombs. Little things that burn fiercely and can't be put out with water.'

The captain looked at him. 'So?'

'They need sand. The Home Guard could have sand on an incendiary ten minutes before a fire engine gets here. We could save dozens of houses, hundreds of lives.'

For a moment the room was silent then broke into a buzz of excited talking. 'Where would we get the sand?'

'There's two miles of the stuff on Hendon Beach, you old fool.'

'Yes, but we can't just have a pile of sand on the street corner?

People would fall over it in the blackout. It would blow away the next windy day we have.'

'Put it in barrels– a large oil drum on each of the main street corners,' Jack said, feeling the excitement.

'Where would we get an oil drum?' someone asked gloomily.

The troop turned to Tommy, as if the boy had all the answers to every problem in Sunderland.

'At the treacle factory at the end of Hendon Road. They have a hundred empty barrels there.'

Everyone smiled, except Jack's granddad.

23

'Will you arrange that, Sergeant Burn?' the captain asked.

'I will, sir,' Granddad said smartly. But he turned to the boys and murmured, 'We could have a little problem there.'

Chapter 4

Sugar and spies

Later that night Granddad stirred the cold ash in his pipe with a penknife while Jack stirred at the coal dust and blew it till it sparked into a feeble flame. 'What's the problem?' he asked.

'The Taylor's Treacle factory buys sugar, turns it into treacle and packs it into barrels.'

Jack frowned. 'We can't get sugar. Not since the war started. Tommy Crawley says it's because the sugar comes in ships and enemy U-boats sink them. Where do Taylor's get the sugar?'

Granddad nodded. 'Good question. The answer is they *don't* get very much sugar these days.'

'So what's in the barrels?' Jack cried.

Granddad held out his pipe and pointed to the bowl. 'That.'

'It's empty.'

'Exactly. And so are the barrels.'

Jack shook his head. 'So they won't mind if we take half a dozen. Why did you say it'll be a problem?'

'Those barrels look like oil barrels,' Granddad said. 'The enemy planes try to hit the factory with bombs—blow up the oil and cause massive damage. When they miss the treacle factory they hit Robinson Terrace, see?'

'The factory should cover them up,' Jack said. 'Somebody should tell them.'

'I did,' Granddad said quietly. 'I went in

my uniform after parade one night. There was a man on guard—a man in a wig. A ginger wig. And he's Welsh.'

Jack frowned. 'Are the Welsh our enemies?'

'They're supposed to be on our side,'

Granddad said, sour as old milk. 'But Wiggy Williams told me it would cost too much money to buy covers for the barrels. Then he went into his hut and came out with a gun. He said if I didn't clear off he'd shoot me. He said I could be an enemy spy.'

'Did you have your rifle, Granddad?' Jack asked. 'Did you shoot him?'

'No, lad, I didn't shoot him. He's mad—mad with power. You give a little man a little job and he thinks he's big enough to look after the crown jewels. He's what we call a "jobsworth"... he says that breaking the rules is more than his job's worth, see?'

Jack took a piece of bread from the table, pushed a fork into it and started to toast it in front of the fire. 'Mad with power. Like Mr Hitler. A sort of Wiggy Hitler.'

'Exactly,' Granddad said.

'So there's no point asking him for a couple of barrels.'

Granddad poked a pipe-cleaner into the stem of his pipe. 'That's why I'm not going to ask him.'

Jack's mouth fell open. 'But you promised. You told the captain you'd get a few barrels. You can't break a promise, Granddad.'

The man looked fierce. 'A Burn never breaks a promise. I said I'd get some barrels and I will. But I won't ask Wiggy Hitler. I'll just take them.'

'A robbery!' the boy cried.

'Not exactly. Those barrels are in prison. I'm going to set them free.'

Jack gave a huge grin. 'You're great, Granddad. You're going to rob an armed guard all on your own?'

'Not exactly,' Granddad said. 'You're coming with me.' And the grin slid off Jack's face like jelly off a playground slide.

Chapter 5
Mates and maps

'I was a sergeant in the last war... the Great War. The best sergeant in the Durham Light Infantry, Colonel Morris said. The best.'

'I know, Granddad.'

'And there's two things made me the best. I'll tell you what they are. First was planning. We knew every shell hole and every trench and every enemy machine gun nest for a mile.'

'And second?'

'Do you know how hunters shoot ducks?'

'Ducks?' Jack laughed.

'They float a wooden duck on the water. The real ducks think there must be food there so they fly down to join it. The hunters shoot the stupid birds.'

'Like sitting ducks,' Jack said. He thought it was a good joke but Granddad wasn't listening.

'The wood models are called "decoy" ducks.'

'We're going to use wooden decoy ducks to fool Wiggy Williams?' Jack asked. He was confused.

'We're going to use a decoy to get Wiggy Williams away from the barrels. That's where you come in.'

'Me?' Jack felt his heart thumping fit to burst out of his chest. Excitement and pride that he'd be helping his granddad and the Home Guard win the war.

'And the third thing is mates,' Granddad began.

'I thought you said there was two things,' Jack cut in.

'There was millions of men fighting in the Great War,' the man went on. 'Even if we

34

never met in the war we all share something. We're mates. And mates do favours.'

'My mate's Tommy Crawley,' Jack said. 'Can he come along?'

'Can you trust him?

'With my life,' Jack said.

'Then he can join the raiding party.'

'Raiding party.' Jack liked the sound of that.

'His dad's a rag and bone man isn't he?'

'Yes, Granddad.'

'Then tell him we'll need his horse and cart at seven tomorrow night.'

Granddad rose to his feet and put the cold pipe in a rack on the mantelpiece. 'I've got this wrist-watch. I need another two watches. One for you and one for Tommy. Then I need to pay a visit to the air-raid post at the end of Hendon Road.' He reached for his overcoat.

'But what's the plan, Granddad?'

'First you get your mate Tommy to look around the barrel yard and draw me a map. Every gate, every wall and every watchman's hut. I know the lad can't read but he can do that, can't he?'

'He's brilliant at drawing,' Jack said, proud of his friend.

'He has to find an excuse to get in there, get past Wiggy Williams, and have a good look round.'

'Can I not do that?' Jack asked.

'No, lad. I have a much more important job for you.'

Jack couldn't stop himself from shaking.

Chapter 6
D.A.F.T. and a duck

The next day dragged on. Jack just wanted night to fall and the raid to start.

Ten minutes to seven, Jack's watch said. Granddad had borrowed the watch from one of the Home Guard troop. Jack carried a torch with tissue paper over the glass so the light didn't show too bright and break the blackout rules. He studied the map one last time.

Tommy Crawley had done a brilliant job. There were twelve rows of ten barrels in a large yard and a guard hut in one corner. In the other corner was a small air-raid shelter.

Tommy had even drawn a picture of Wiggy Williams and used coloured crayons to shade it. Orange hair stuck out from under a blue tin helmet. Little wire-rimmed spectacles sat on a button nose. The cheeks were a hot red and the moustache small as a toothbrush.

On the other side of the paper Jack studied the words he had to learn. 'The Defence Against Factory Targets group.'

Tommy sat on the driving seat of his dad's stinking rag and bone cart, hidden in the dark back lane alongside the treacle factory.

Granddad stood in the shadows of the grocer's shop doorway opposite the high wooden gates of the treacle factory. There was a bright enough moon to see quite clearly. The gates were painted blue with white letters that read, 'Taylor's Tasty Treacle For Toffee And Tarts.' Those blue gates were tall as a double-decker bus but there was a small door set in the side of them.

Five minutes to seven. Granddad gave a soft quacking

sound. That was the signal for Jack the decoy duck to start his part of the plan.

Jack walked across the road and hammered on the door in the gates. He began to shout, 'Mr Williams... Mr Williams, open up. Mr Will-iiii-aaaa-ms!'

There was the sound of the guard hut

door opening and boots clattering across the yard. 'Who's there?' a squeaky voice with a Welsh accent called from behind the door.

'I'm Arthur Levy,' Jack replied, borrowing the name of an uncle in Newcastle.

'Go away or I'll shoot you. I've got a pistol here.'

'I have an urgent message from the Defence Against Factory Targets group.'

'Who?'

'D.A.F.T.'

'Daft? I'm not daft.'

'But I am,' Jack replied. It was four minutes to seven. 'I'm a runner for the special Defence Against Factory Targets team. You must have heard of us.'

'Never. Push off. I've got a machine gun aimed at the door.'

'The people at D.A.F.T. have spies in Europe. We've just had a report that Sunderland is the target for an air raid tonight.'

'What's that to do with me?' the guard behind the blue gate asked.

'The Taylor's Treacle factory is the main target. The enemy scout planes reported your barrels looked like barrels full of oil. Your yard will be wiped out at five past seven o'clock—in eight minutes' time.'

'I'll believe it when I hear the air-raid siren, and I'll be in my shelter,' the man said.

'You don't understand,' Jack groaned. This was harder than he'd thought. 'If a dozen bombs land in your yard you'll be blown to mincemeat. You have to get a mile away to the shelter in Mowbray Road.'

'I'll leave when I hear the siren,' the

stubborn man said. 'This is my duty. No siren, no go. More than my job's worth.'

Jack wailed, 'It will be too late then. The siren will go at seven exactly. The bombers arrive at five minutes past seven. It's two minutes to seven now. You have seven minutes to save yourself.'

'If them sirens sound at seven I'll have

five minutes. I can run a mile in five minutes. Top-class sprinter for Wales I was, son.'

'It's not *if* the sirens go. The siren *will* sound at seven,' Jack cried. The boy knew that because Granddad had arranged it with his mates in the Air Raid offices. There were plenty of false air-raid warnings. One more wouldn't matter.

Then something happened that Jack didn't expect.

Chapter 7
Sirens and shelters

The air-raid sirens began to wail. They were not supposed to start till seven o'clock exactly. That was why they had all checked their watches so carefully. Now everything would be rushed.

The little door in the gate flew open and a face poked out. The face looked exactly like Tommy's picture. 'You were right, boy. I'll just lock up,' he said and stepped out.

'No!' Jack cried. 'They are using high explosives. The blast will blow the walls down, and flying bricks could blow half of Hendon Road away.'

'What am I supposed to do?'

'Open the main gates wide. The blast will escape and do no harm.'

'Really?'

'Really—it's the D.A.F.T. thing to do,' the boy told him.

As Wiggy Williams struggled with bolts to throw open the main gates, Jack looked up into the purple skies. Searchlights sent their pencil beams up into the air. Barrage balloons glittered silver and floated in the breeze like kites on steel cables—cables that would wreck any bomber that tried to fly too low.

Jack smiled across the road to where he knew Granddad was waiting in the dark doorway. The timing may have been two minutes early but everything else was

wonderful. Granddad's mates had put on a wonderful show.

Then Jack frowned. As the sirens wailed on he heard another sound. The sound of aircraft engines. Jack shook his head in wonder. How had Granddad made that happen? Did he have mates in the enemy air force?

As Wiggy Williams vanished down the street, Granddad appeared at Jack's side. 'Don't stand there like a can of milk, lad. There's an air raid on.'

'No there isn't. It's a decoy,' Jack argued.

The Sunderland gunners sent streams of shells into the sky to try and hit the enemy bombers that were droning louder and closer. 'Of course it's not a decoy,' Granddad groaned.

He gave a sharp whistle and Tommy Crawley brought his dad's cart clattering round the corner and stopped in front

of the open gates. The horse was stamping and sparking its iron shoes on the cobbles, afraid of the noise and flashing lights. Jack held the reins while Tommy went to help Granddad roll barrels out of the treacle factory yard.

'We have to get to a shelter!' Tommy called.

People were running down the street and heading for their nearest shelter, quiet and clutching at blankets, children with their favourite toys and some women still pinning their hats on. No one took any notice of the robbers.

'No point going to the shelter. If a bomb has our name on it then it'll get us. It'll find us if we are in a shelter or riding a rag and bone man's cart. Now help us get this last one on the back,' Granddad grunted.

At last the fourth barrel was on the cart. Explosions made the air tremble and fires erupted from the shipyards. Tommy slapped the reins and the horse shot off

down Hendon Road. He laughed. 'It's like one of the cowboy films at the Marina cinema on a Saturday morning. We're the wagon train racing to the safety of the fort.'

'You're crackers,' Jack shouted over the crashing of hooves and clatter of barrels.

'I may be crackers,' Tommy said, 'but you're D.A.F.T.'

Chapter 8
Looting and saluting

When the Home Guard met the next night in the church hall they were smeared with red paint and caked in sand but looked smug. A barrel stood at the end of the four main roads and each one was full of sand.

'There was a lot of damage in the docks last night,' the captain said. 'And the church in Tower Street burned down before the fire brigade could get there.'

'There'll be a barrel of sand handy next time the fire bombs fall on Hendon,' Granddad said quietly.

The captain tucked a corner of his moustache into his mouth and sucked. 'It seems a Mr Williams—a guard at the treacle factory—says there were four barrels stolen from the yard last night. Looters broke in while the raid was on. The punishment for looting is a very long spell in jail.'

The men looked at their paint-stained hands and tried to rub them clean. 'Four miserable empty barrels?' Granddad muttered.

'Worth two pounds each,' the captain said. The men shook their heads in sorrow.

There was a sharp rap at the door and a policeman walked in. 'Good evening, gentlemen,' he said. His face was hard as

teak wood as he let his sharp eyes slowly scan the room. The eyes rested on Jack.

'There has been a report of a theft of some barrels,' he said.

'What colour?' Tommy Crawley asked.

The policeman pulled a notebook from his pocket and looked at it. 'Blue, with white writing saying "Taylor's Treacle".'

The Home Guard shook their heads.

'Haven't seen any blue barrels, have we, lads?' the captain asked.

'All I have is a report of a boy who was sent as a decoy. A small boy with a thin, pointed nose and ears like jug handles.' The constable's eyes rested on Jack again for a moment. 'This jug-eared boy claimed to be from a group called...' He looked at his notebook again. 'Defence Against Factory Targets.'

'That's daft,' Jack said, blushing and giggling in terror because he knew he'd been caught.

'What's your name, sonny?' the policeman growled.

'Jack Burn.'

'Ah,' the policeman sighed. 'The decoy boy was called Arthur Levy.'

'It can't have been our Jack, then,' Granddad said.

The policeman nodded. 'So no one has seen four blue barrels? And no one had heard of this boy Arthur?'

'No one.'

'And can you explain the red paint on your hands?' the constable asked.

'We've been painting windows with red paint instead of making blackout curtains,' the captain said.

'Of course you have, sir.' The policeman's face almost cracked into a smile.

He saluted and turned to go. Granddad followed him to the door.

'How have you been since the Great War, Cecil?' Granddad asked him.

'Fine thanks to you, Sergeant Burn. I'll never forget you saved my life. They should have given you a medal for that.'

'I was just doing my job. You were in my platoon. I had to look after you.'

The policeman stepped into the cool evening air. 'I owe you.'

The two men stood silent for a long while. Finally Granddad said, 'And this case of the stolen barrels?'

'I believe it may have been a criminal gang from South Shields. I will tell my chief inspector to drop the case.' He glanced back through the door at Jack. 'I will stop looking for a boy calling himself Arthur Levy and I believe this Defence Against Factory Targets group is nonsense.'

'Plain daft,' Granddad agreed.

The policeman tapped his helmet in a salute again then held out his hand to shake Granddad's. 'Good night Sergeant Burn—the best sergeant in the Durham Light Infantry. The best.'

'I tell our Jack that,' the man said. 'So you're off on patrol now?'

The policeman looked at his hand. 'As soon as I've rubbed this red paint off.'

Granddad looked at his own stained hand. 'Sorry about that, Cecil.'

The policeman sighed. 'We don't want

people thinking I've been painting stolen blue barrels red, do we?'

And he walked off into the thick gloom, whistling.

Epilogue

The granddad in this true story was upset when the Second World War started. He was told he was too old to fight. He said he would dye his grey hair and lie to say he was younger. But the dye went wrong and he ended up with bright red hair.

He joined the Home Guard and was annoyed when an air raid missed a store of barrels and damaged his street. He was sure the bomber was aiming for the barrels and believed they were oil drums. Granddad wanted them moved. They could be spread around the town as sand bins to put out fires.

The owner of the barrels refused to give them away. Granddad decided to use his skills from the First World War to organise a raid and steal them. They were quickly painted red and filled with sand.

The red paint didn't fool anybody but the police didn't bother taking the thieves to court. Even the owner of the barrels knew who had stolen them but decided it wasn't worth making a fuss about it after all.

The sand bins stood on the street corners for five years till the war was over. There was never another raid on those streets and the sand was never needed.

But Granddad felt he had done his best to help Britain to win the war with his great barrel burglary.

Terry Deary
World War II Tales

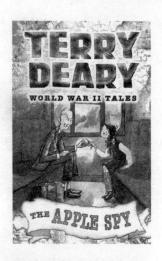

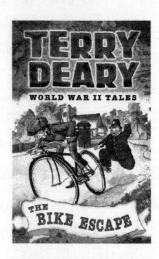

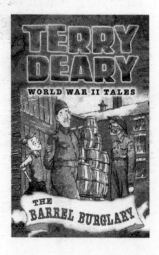

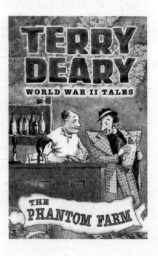